THE DAY
THE WORLD DIED

THE DAY
THE WORLD DIED

THE GREATEST PARADIGM SHIFT IN HUMANITY

K.D. MCPHEE

© 2019 by Bishop King David McPhee
THE DAY THE WORLD DIED by K. D. McPhee

Printed in the USA

ISBN

All rights reserved solely by the author. The author guarantees all contents are original and do not infringe upon the legal rights of any other person or work. No part of this book may be reproduced in any form without the permission of the author. The views expressed in this book are not necessarily those of the publisher.

Graphic Illustrator: kleinsdesignz@gmail.com

Author's Photo: Rodger D. Productions – Nassau, Bahamas

Contents

DEDICATION 7

ACKNOWLEDGMENTS 9

INTRODUCTION 11

Chapter 1 Manuscripts Of Ancient Prophets 13

Chapter 2 The Journey Of A Lifetime 17

Chapter 3 A Day Foretold By My Father 21

Chapter 4 The Day Of Cleansing 27

Chapter 5 A Cataclysmic Disaster 31

Chapter 6 The Greatest Paradigm Shift In Human Experience ..35

Chapter 7 Immortalization Initiation 39

Chapter 8 The Reward Ceremony 43

Chapter 9 My New Place Of "Soul Rest" 47

Dedication

Growing up in a rural community such as Betsy Bay, Mayaguana, and to dream of becoming a writer was far beyond my wildest dream. I was encouraged to dream as big as I could, which I did simply because I believed that dreams turned into action can be realized.

This book is dedicated to my late father and first mentor, Rev. David McPhee. Daddy, I told you that one day I would make you proud and, believe it or not, that day is finally here. I know that you are looking down from Heaven's Balcony cheering me on.

I reminisce on the many days you and I were alone on the ocean and you spoke the words of hope and expectation deep into my spirit. Your life was an example of faith and hope for me. Often times it appeared as if you had a good reason to give up and throw in the towel, but you didn't. I can see you now as your bruised hands clasped the oar and struck the pine until it made so many revolutions that even I thought the boat had an engine. I am thankful to you, Daddy, for your Godly advice and commitment to God and family. I've watched you struggle, yet you overcame many obstacles. Your community mindedness has taught me how to serve for the greater good rather than for the greater gain.

Thank you Daddy for the chastisement I received from your hands and the scolding from your lips. Your method of correction obviously worked; although I was not a fan back then, I certainly appreciate its impact now.

Anyway Daddy, I must go now as I have to "feed the goats" (that's our secret). I will see you next time with volume II of "The Day the World Died."

Thanks Daddy,

Your son David…

Acknowledgments

There comes a time in the eternal scheme of things when an idea cannot be stopped when its time has come to fruition. This book is such an idea. The divine plane of the Father of Light has afforded me to pen these words so the world will know that there is a Universal System at work.

I want to acknowledge the power of the Spirit of God that has given me the impetus to write such a book. Without His guidance, it could not be done. When I look back and consider this body of work, it amazes me to see the creative language and thought pattern that His Spirit has expressed through me. Thank You Father for trusting me with this work.

To my greatest human support and encouragement, my beautiful wife of 26 years, Dorothy McPhee. Honey you were there for me in good times and bad. There were many days when I felt I could not finish this work, but you encouraged me to continue. Even when I felt alone because of the attacks that came against me, you prayed for me and for the success of this project. I want to thank you for your overwhelming love and support. I am who I am today because you spoke to the "King" in me.

To my children: Inga, David, Delano, Davinchi, Tiny, Shelby and KJ. Thank you so much for your prayers and love. You guys are the wind beneath my wings, and I love you to the moon and back. One day you will look back and show your children all that we have done. Thank you guys!

Introduction

There is nothing like having the freedom to be creative and able to dream a little. Not long ago I had a dream about **The Day The World Died**. I take you back to my childhood days when I took an unforgettable trip to one of our family islands called Mayaguana in the Bahamas. It is a popular stopover for boaters on a direct route to the eastern Caribbean.

The story tells how I accidently stumbled on an old piece of torn literature and carefully opened its pages and began reading. Surprisingly the pages contained the ancient teachings of the prophets. They spoke of a coming Redeemer who would rescue the human race from its selfishness.

Ancient prophets were specially prepared by God for a very special ministry. They brought divine words to people who desperately needed to hear it. Though they lived many years ago and were speaking to a group of people who are no longer here, their words are still valuable to us today and we can see the present day applications of the messages they delivered.

In the ancient manuscript we were prepared to experience paradise. Instead we got paradise squared. We were asked to get use to our eternalized bodies. Instead, we were taken to a secluded area where all immortals were told to exercise our deathlessness. To exercise one's deathlessness was to be sure of his eternalness. The indestructible body was one to be admired because of the vastness of its knowledge base.

I share how we knew all things because of our conscious connection to the infinite mind of our Creator. In this new realization there was no time for contemplating. The information we needed to function was not to be recalled, for to recall was an action for the old consciousness. Living in this experience cannot be fully explained, because it has to be lived to understand the joy that is so real until it feels like it could be cut with a knife.

The conclusion of this fiction is that there is no progression of time in this new reality, because time was a well spent former commodity. In the eternal scheme of things, the Creator always desired that His people would be eternalized. In the time belt, choice was given to the human creation to reveal the righteousness of our leader - the King of all kings and Lord of all lords.

Chapter 1

Manuscripts of Ancient Prophets

While reaching for the lantern on the top shelf, I accidently stumbled on an old piece of literature. I turned the flame up on the lantern but its aging flame barely provided the glow that I needed. I was grateful for any amount of flame I was allowed to enjoy.

To my surprise the literature was battered and torn from its use or abuse. My first thought was to reach down and gather every little piece and give it to father; it was probably his anyway. On second thought, I carefully opened its pages and began reading. Surprisingly the pages contained the ancient teachings of the prophets. They spoke of a coming Redeemer who would rescue the human race from its selfishness.

Ancient prophets were specially prepared by God for a very special ministry. They brought divine words to people who desperately needed to hear it. Though they lived many years ago and were speaking to a group of people who are no longer here, their words are still valuable to us today and we can see the present day applications of the messages they delivered. In ancient days we see God spoke to Moses concerning those who prophesy in the name of the LORD.

> Deut. 18:18-22
> *I will raise up for them a prophet like you from among their fellow Israelites, and I will put my words in his mouth. He will tell them everything I command him. 19 I myself will call to account anyone who does not listen to my words that the prophet speaks in my name. 20 But a prophet who presumes to speak in my name anything I have not commanded, or a prophet who speaks in the name of other gods, is to be put to death. 21 You may say to yourselves, "How can we know when a message has not been spoken by the Lord?" 22 If what a prophet proclaims in the name of the Lord does not take place or come true, that is a message the Lord has not spoken. That prophet has spoken presumptuously, so do not be alarmed.*

God took the idea of prophecy seriously and He expected those called to do the same. He also expected those receiving the words of a prophet to listen and obey, because they were worthy of death if they abused their calling. It revealed the seriousness of the voice of a prophet during ancient times.

The Finalization Of Immortalization
As I began reading the writings of ancient prophets, I noticed the lantern had just given its last glimmer. I realized that more time had lapsed than I had expected.

While stashing the book away, I realized the idea of the finalization of the immortalization of the human race would eventually be completed by this Redeemer.

Immortalization is living forever and never dying. A person's soul is said to be immortal. The Bible clearly teaches a continuing existence after death for all. For believers this will be deathless and imperishable, marked by that glory and honour that comes from union with Christ.

Since immortality is now obscured in corruptible bodies, changes will occur. Believers will have appropriately different bodies; their immortality will be evident. This fact, along with the bodily resurrection, Paul sees as assured because of the Spirit's guarantee, the defeat of death, and the ultimate victory of God through Jesus Christ.

> 1 Cor. 15:54-57
> *When the perishable has been clothed with the imperishable, and the mortal with immortality, then the saying that is written will come true: "Death has been swallowed up in victory." 55 "Where, O death, is your victory? Where, O death, is your sting?" 56 The sting of death is sin, and the power of sin is the law. 57 But thanks be to God! He gives us the victory through our Lord Jesus Christ.*

> I Tim. 6:13-16
> *In the sight of God, who gives life to everything, and of Christ Jesus, who while testifying before Pontius Pilate made the good confession, I charge you 14 to keep this command without spot or blame until the appearing*

of our Lord Jesus Christ, 15 which God will bring about in his own time—God, the blessed and only Ruler, the King of kings and Lord of lords, 16 who alone is immortal and who lives in unapproachable light, whom no one has seen or can see. To him be honour and might forever. Amen.

The truth is: God is beyond all the positions of power and authority. He cannot be defined or confined by any other person's plans or purposes. He is the Creator of all other persons; the only immortal, invisible, eternal King of all things.

CHAPTER 2

The Journey of a Lifetime

Immediately before my feet touched the floor, I was reminded by the lovely Mayaguana family island view in the Bahamas that there existed much more spiritual essence than we were told. I always knew as a boy that there was more to life than I ever realized.

The sleepy village of Betsy Bay Mayaguana was awakened by the sound of roosters crowing and birds chirping. The sound was almost alarming. The smell of the ocean was very obnoxious. I really did not understand the mixed smell and sound of that particular morning.

Mayaguana - A Family Island In The Bahamas
Mayaguana is the easternmost island and district of the Bahamas. Its population was 277 in the 2010 census. It has an area of about 280 km2 (110 sq mi) and is 560 km (350 mi) southeast of the capital Nassau. Mayaguana is considered the halfway point between South Florida and Puerto Rico and is about 830 km (520

mi) off Palm Beach, Florida. It is a popular stopover for boaters on a direct route to the eastern Caribbean.

It is believed Mayaguana was also one of the first islands that Christopher Columbus landed on during his journey to the new world. The largest settlement is Abraham's Bay (pop. 143) on the south coast; other settlements are the neighbouring towns of Betsy Bay (pop. 44) and Pirate's Well (pop. 90) in the northwest with the population slowly decreasing. The uninhabited areas of Upper Point (north shore), Northeast Point, and Southeast Point are largely inaccessible by road.

An Unforgettable Trip
My father called me to make preparation for our trip to Northwest Point to collect conch (sea muscle); a Bahamian delicacy. I was reluctant to prepare myself for the journey; something just didn't feel right about this time. We must have made this trip about a thousand times. Nevertheless, my father gathered the necessary things needed for the trip.

We set sail very early that morning with a sharp northwestern breeze which challenged our progress. The waves slapped against the side of the fifteen feet boat that we had used to make this journey so many times. My father seemed worried but he tried hiding it from me. I knew him too well to believe that all was well.

Looking deep into his eyes, I noticed that he had aged. The sagging skin that lined his cheek bone told the story of many disappointments. I never thought that this patriarch would look so frail. His once huge muscles were now a victim of gravity. I watched him labour with tremendous congregational burdens throughout many years. He would tell me stories of his early child hood, and I always looked forward to those stories because they were very interesting.

This time I could not ignore how loud the silence was, it was so loud until it drowned the sound of the angry waves. At the same time the sun started to peep from behind the morning clouds that seemed unsure whether to expose the sun or wrap it in her bosom for yet another day.

The weather started to deteriorate so much so that my Father suggested that we sailed into the harbour for safety. After a few minutes of trying to shift our sailing position we eventually accomplished this most daunting task. Upon disembarkation I recognized that we were not alone, several mariners who were known to us had already suffered loss with respect to the threatening storm. This so called safe harbour was nothing more than a sandy bank surrounded by miles of grape trees.

The senior mariners asked us younger sailors to make a fire to keep our selves warm. However, this presented a big challenge because of the nature of the terrain. The wind swirled around the palm trees as if she was dancing to be set free from some unforeseen force. We somehow managed to kindle a fire. My father waived to the other mariners to join us by the fire for better warmth. It was during this time that I also noticed fear on the faces of the other sailors. The day was far spent worrying about our families as to what will become of them in this unexpected bad weather.

Dusk fell upon us rather quickly. All of us were too pre-occupied with the task of worrying; hence, we missed the fleeting moments. Darkness engulfed us while my father was speaking to the group concerning the ancient manuscript. He reminded us of how some humans believed that they would not be held accountable for their actions. I fixed my gaze on his face noticing how the image was unclear because of the scarce light from the fire. This effect had created a silhouette.

Drops of rain fell softly on the leaves making melody so sweet until I almost faded off to sleep. My father's voice soothed the many troubled hearts that surrounded the almost extinguished fire. Some of the mariners fell asleep. I somehow surprisingly stayed awake to hear the remainder of my father's conversation.

Chapter 3

A Day Foretold by my Father

I recall most of my life in ministry with my father where I would hear him speak of a day that would come when the human race would be called into account for our earthly occupancy.

The evening dragged on and my father finally told me of the horrible day of cleansing that was inevitable. At that time the rain started pouring, the sky appeared as if it was about to release mud. The darkness was so thick until using a knife to cut it seemed appropriate.

There was confusion everywhere; the wind increased her forward speed. The earth shook lightly while my father held me tightly. His grip felt as if fear had taken control; not fear of dying, but fear of losing the eternal soul. He told me he knew this day would come but not so soon. Softly he said to me, "Son, this is it - it has begun".

Some of the other mariners had been screaming for help, but it was too dark to even see our hands in front of us. The wind and rain took their toll on all of our bodies. My heart was racing feverishly because of the impending reality of finding some of the mariners dead.

Again, my father pulled me close to him, pressing my face to his. His breath was faint, the words he spoke cut through my heart like a hot knife through butter. I will never forget the sound of these words: "Son, prepare your own self to transition from this world to the other; I am dying son."

The Day Of Cleansing Had Begin
After shaking him violently, I finally realized he was gone. I looked around for the other mariners and got no response after screaming all their names. I came to the cold reality that the 'Day Of Cleansing' had begun.

The New Testament emphasizes that, although the Old Testament rituals were of benefit in showing people the seriousness of sin, they could not in themselves remove sin. They were only a temporary arrangement. Now that Christ has come, they are of no further use.

> Hebrews 9:6-10
> *When everything had been arranged like this, the priests entered regularly into the outer room to carry on their ministry. 7 But only the high priest entered the inner room, and that only once a year, and never without blood, which he offered for himself and for the sins the people had committed in ignorance. 8 The Holy Spirit was showing by this that the way into the Most Holy Place had not yet been disclosed as long as the first tabernacle was still functioning. 9 This is*

an illustration for the present time, indicating that the gifts and sacrifices being offered were not able to clear the conscience of the worshiper. 10 They are only a matter of food and drink and various ceremonial washings—external regulations applying until the time of the new order.

Heb. 9:11-14. The Blood of Christ
But when Christ came as high priest of the good things that are now already here, he went through the greater and more perfect tabernacle that is not made with human hands, that is to say, is not a part of this creation. 12 He did not enter by means of the blood of goats and calves; but he entered the Most Holy Place once for all by his own blood, thus obtaining[b] eternal redemption. 13 The blood of goats and bulls and the ashes of a heifer sprinkled on those who are ceremonially unclean sanctify them so that they are outwardly clean. 14 How much more, then, will the blood of Christ, who through the eternal Spirit offered himself unblemished to God, cleanse our consciences from acts that lead to death,[c] so that we may serve the living God!

His one sacrifice has done what all the Israelite sacrifices could not do.

Heb. 10:11-12
Day after day every priest stands and performs his religious duties; again and again he offers the same sacrifices, which can never take away sins. 12 But when this priest had offered for all time one sacrifice for sins, he sat down at the right hand of God,

Entrance into the presence of God, which was restricted under the Old Testament system, is now available to all God's people through their high priest, Jesus Christ.

> Heb. 10:19-22 A Call to Persevere in Faith
> *Therefore, brothers and sisters, since we have confidence to enter the Most Holy Place by the blood of Jesus, 20 by a new and living way opened for us through the curtain, that is, his body, 21 and since we have a great priest over the house of God, 22 let us draw near to God with a sincere heart and with the full assurance that faith brings, having our hearts sprinkled to cleanse us from a guilty conscience and having our bodies washed with pure water.*

> Heb. 9:8
> *The Holy Spirit was showing by this that the way into the Most Holy Place had not yet been disclosed as long as the first tabernacle was still functioning.*

When the Israelite high priest had completed the sin-cleansing rituals in the tabernacle-tent, he reappeared to the people. Likewise Jesus Christ, having dealt with sin fully and having obtained eternal forgiveness for sins will reappear to bring his people's salvation to its glorious climax.

> Heb. 9:12; Heb. 9:28
> *He did not enter by means of the blood of goats and calves; but he entered the Most Holy Place once for all by his own blood, thus obtaining[a] eternal redemption.*

28 so Christ was sacrificed once to take away the sins of many; and he will appear a second time, not to bear sin, but to bring salvation to those who are waiting for him.

Through this tragic ordeal, I was also injured but alive. I remembered praying and asking for guidance. All the elements were wildly colliding so much until it seemed like a power struggle was being pursued. Then I remembered hearing how my father spoke of what will take place at the beginning of the cleansing. He said darkness and confusion would be at first, but not for those who followed the teachings of the manuscript.

There was hardly any time for mourning. I followed the narrow path that led to a cross road. That track road was almost impossible to pass because of the many boulders blocking its path. A flash of lightning showed me the way around. I felt myself shifting from one reality to another. My consciousness was very unstable. However, I tried to remain focused on finding more survivors.

Chapter 4
The Day of Cleansing

The *Day Of Cleansing* was devastating as it gave rise to a new consciousness. This new reality stirred the curiosity of the modern truth seekers. One group of seekers believed in linear travel, while others believed in cyclic travel. The cyclic view was that the world would not come to an end. Instead, life would continue to go around. On the other hand, the linear view was that the world would come to an end. They believed that the world was destined to systematically collapse.

For centuries advanced souls looked forward to a spiritual leader who would eradicate social injustice and religious dogma and usher us into a new world system; one that would lift the down trodden and equalize the marginalized. This super spiritualized leader was written about in the ancient manuscript by the Major and Minor Prophets.

The climax of an age of human suffering and degradation had begun. The sun went down with a burning glow scorching across the sky with a degree of vengeance. People were panicking everywhere. Nearby I gazed into the eyes of a mother who was clutching onto her little young child. it was evident that fear was her constant companion. Sweat poured down her face that was already streaked with the daunting story of her life.

The earth shook one more time. Houses were moved off their foundations, while others were simply swallowed up by the massive quake. The darkness of the night filled the entire square, as if she too was searching for a hiding place. The familiar sounds of crickets and night bugs were overwhelmed by the agonizing sound of people shouting for help.

There was a flash light in my possession. Apparently I had packed it in my overnight bag the night before going on a hunting trip. I quickly retrieved it from my overnighter and tested it; thank God it worked. While searching for survivors, my strength and courage started to slowly dwindle. Just before giving up I heard a faint sound, at first it sounded like a wailing hooping owl, but as I drew closer it sounded like someone crying: "Help! Help"!

Victims Of The Most Horrific Disaster In Human History
The sound echoed throughout the entire atmosphere sending reminders of the severity and urgency of this tragic disaster. I scrambled in the midst of the rubble to retrieve an unknown stranger. However, we all had one thing in common: we were victims of the most horrific disaster in human history.

I shined the light on the area where the wailing sound came from and discovered a woman hanging on for dear life to the branch of a tree. There was a gaping hole in the earth just beneath her. I stretched forth my hand to rescue her as she vigorously grabbed my hand. I pulled her out with every ounce of energy left in my body. The earth had reclaimed her possessions; things that were material in nature. My heart was racing as I wondered where and when would the next devastation take place.

Matt. 24:36 The Day and Hour Unknown
But about that day or hour no one knows, not even the angels in heaven, nor the Son, but only the Father.

The sky seemed to be giving us warnings by speaking a language that was foreign to the human race. The stars were few and almost no-existent. Night clouds appeared to be sketches of ancient drawings similar to that which was foretold by the Old Testament Prophet Daniel.

Daniel chapter 12: The End Times
At that time Michael, the great prince who protects your people, will arise. There will be a time of distress such as has not happened from the beginning of nations until then. But at that time your people—everyone whose name is found written in the book—will be delivered. 2 Multitudes who sleep in the dust of the earth will awake: some to everlasting life, others to shame and everlasting contempt. 3 Those who are wise will shine like the brightness of the heavens, and those who lead many to righteousness, like the stars for ever and ever. 4 But you, Daniel, roll up and seal the words of the scroll until the time of the end. Many will go here and there to increase knowledge." 5 Then I, Daniel, looked, and there before me stood two others, one on this bank of the river and one on the opposite bank. 6 One of them said to the man clothed in linen, who was above the waters of the river, "How long will it be before these astonishing things are fulfilled?" 7 The man clothed in linen, who was above the waters of the river, lifted his right hand and his left hand toward heaven, and I heard him swear by him who

lives forever, saying, "It will be for a time, times and half a time. When the power of the holy people has been finally broken, all these things will be completed." 8 I heard, but I did not understand. So I asked, "My lord, what will the outcome of all this be?" 9 He replied, "Go your way, Daniel, because the words are rolled up and sealed until the time of the end. 10 Many will be purified, made spotless and refined, but the wicked will continue to be wicked. None of the wicked will understand, but those who are wise will understand. 11 "From the time that the daily sacrifice is abolished and the abomination that causes desolation is set up, there will be 1,290 days. 12 Blessed is the one who waits for and reaches the end of the 1,335 days. 13 "As for you, go your way till the end. You will rest, and then at the end of the days you will rise to receive your allotted inheritance.

The wind rustled through the trees ripping branches and destroying underbrush. Death was evident all around me. I said to myself: This must be the beginning of the apocalypse.

Chapter 5
A Cataclysmic Disaster

This geographical shock left me pulling myself together as my sense of balance eroded. I picked up a hand held radio very quickly to dial Weather Central. To my surprise the voice that responded seemed desponded, static and almost artificial. Immediately I realized it was a recording. It said:

> "Obviously if you are hearing this message - the world would have already experience it's most horrendous and cataclysmic disaster better known as the apocalypse."

Merriam-Webster dictionary defines an apocalypse as: one of the Jewish and Christian writings of 200 b.c. to a.d. 150 marked by pseudonymity, symbolic imagery, and the expectation of an imminent cosmic cataclysm in which God destroys the ruling powers of evil and raises the righteous to life in a messianic kingdom.

The Christian end-of-the-world story is part of the revelation in John of Patmos' book "Apokalypsis" meaning "a cataclysmic event".

The fully apocalyptic visions in Daniel chapters 7–12, as well as those in the New Testament's Revelation, can trace their roots to pre-exile latter biblical prophets; the sixth century BCE prophets Ezekiel, Isaiah (chapters 40–55 and 56–66), Haggai 2, and Zechariah 1–8 show a transition phase between prophecy and apocalyptic ...

Scores of people were missing. Young babies were ripped out of their mother's arms. Families were displaced, hope was scarce; a young boy shouted to the top of his voce:

"There is no more sea and the river has dried up".
The old man gasping for breath cried, "What do you mean by that?" He too had suffered a head blow from a fast moving boulder. The rivers and swamps all seemed too have dried up. Night dragged on painfully while we discovered more survivors. The expectancy of seeing the sun seemed far-fetched. Nevertheless, morning came with a yellow beam of hope for the human race. The sun shined brightly while dancing across the sky to the tune of a gentle eastern breeze carrying with her a splendour that was never seen before.

Between System Failure And Things To Come
It was because of this apocalyptic occurrence that there was a shift in human consciousness. The old system had collapsed and governments around the world had failed. It appeared as if no one had the answers to poignant issues. We were between a system of failure and things to come. The human race was struggling to survive. Hope was scarce; everyone did what they could to help a troubled race of people.

The following were observed after the collapse of the old system:
- No organized movement of people, goods, or services.
- Social injustice became prevalent among us.
- Hunger and violence seemed normal.
- Wrong became right and right became wrong.

There was an intensity of social decadence never experienced among us before. Finding copies of the old manuscript was near impossible; those writings pointed us toward the light.

Everyone took heed to the words of the manuscript before the darkness took hold of our race. As for darkness; this destroyer of the human soul made fathers turn against sons, mothers against daughters, husbands against wives, families against families. Eventually zone wars were experienced. This epidemic of violence further destroyed our young people; the young men in particular.

The promises of a young Jewish leader
After the failure of civilization, some of the aged men, who had great knowledge of the manuscript, set up groups of people interested in hearing about the promises of a young Jewish leader.

Centuries before our time It was said that the young leader had made several bold claims that collided with his elders at the time. Some of his claims were beyond the capacity of the religious intellect of His day. Here are a few:

- He claimed that he would give up his life to the greatest enemy of the human race which was death.
- He also claimed that he would regain his life after three days.
- He further claimed that he would be taken away from our planet, but he would return to take away his people to a better place that was prepared for those who believed his claims.

the aged men who we left among us taught these promises to all who would hear.

As time progressed, we who accepted these promises noticed a difference in our behaviour. We were being changed from a place on the inside of our consciousness. We met daily for prayers and talks from our elders. They told us that soon we would be free from all the violence and despair that was all around us. However, some days were extremely difficult to see our love ones swallowed up by the destructive culture of greed and rebellion.

CHAPTER 6

The Greatest Paradigm Shift in Human Experience

The evening of the greatest shift in human experience took place during our worship time by the banks of the river. We realized something was changing; it was an inward change taking place.

From Mortal To Immortal
We had experienced the shift from mortal to immortal. We quickly realized this supernatural event was the beginning of what was promised to us by our leader thousands of years ago. We were told by the elders to release ourselves from all thoughts of things that were material in nature and embrace the new experience of Spirit.

Almost instantaneously and miraculously our consciousness shifted toward the new system. This new way of thinking was ushered in unconsciously; nevertheless, we embraced the new paradigm shift. There was a sense of righteousness all around the planet. We all had a new mandate, Righteousness and perfection became our cultural icons. Teams of qualified individuals were selected to survey the entire global hemisphere. This quest was mandated by the new council responsible for the orderly movement of transformed humans, now known as the immortals.

In human expression and measure of time, it felt as if it took two weeks for this disaster to complete itself. But in the new reality it amounts to one day. The true purpose for the shift in human consciousness was to neutralize time; causing it to dissolve brought about a new reality.

Memory of the old way of life was erased. People came together for the good of brotherhood among the new species of earth dwellers. We now live in societies freed from strife, war and confusion. It was always our fate to live void of any opposing forces. The cosmos breathed a clean sigh of relief after the cleansing process.

Middle earth had survived her greatest catastrophe ever known to its inhabitants. Nature regained her balance. The destabilization of the ocean floor caused the beaches to erode almost to the point of non-existence. We had entered a new reality of not having time-related experiences. Time was eradicated by His Majesty.

Crowning Of A New World Leader
The new world leader was crowned king of the new race of immortals. We were all summoned to the crowning ceremony. It took flashes of eternity to get used to the new bodies. Our King of the new race of immortals sat on His throne which was elevated high above all living things. The splendour of his majesty was seen throughout the entire galaxy.

We had no need for the sun in this new reality. I looked around and it seemed almost unreal to be experiencing such joy that was never known to the old race. We were made aware of our celestial arrangements according to our rank and file.

Every immortal that belonged to the Saint Peters' block was place on the second level of empty space. It appeared as if we were floating along the Milky Way, for there was no place found for our feet. Yet we were resting on solid nothingness.

Immortals were worshiping everywhere. There was a feeling of fulfilment in the stratosphere. We wept but there was no saline found. The one who had the nail pressed hands told us in the ancient manuscript that there will be no more tears. This was proven to be true because even though immortals cried, there was no saline found.

The messiah had abolished time, death, hell, and the grave. He deemed them hazardous, useless, and most of all, something that was too memorable to the old consciousness.

Glorious New Bodies In A New City
We all had new bodies. These new vessels were glorious; they would reach maximum speed of twice the velocity of light and quadruple the speed of sound.

Living in this new reality felt like utopia. In this new society with its walls reinforced with righteousness, and the standard of conduct is holiness, there really was no place found for the occupancy of injustice. The human race as we knew it had been extinct. The free movement of evil that was allowed to permeate the consciousness of the old race had caused them the opportunity to reside in the celestial city.

Many humans that I knew did not make it to the shores of the immortal city. It was a tragedy they had encountered because of their greed and selfishness. They all perished on the day of cleansing.

It was very difficult to recall life in the old reality. The only way to measure our frequency of congregating was by the sound of harps playing celestial harmonies at certain intervals, because time was something of old which remained in the abyss of the lost human race.

The new city was one of clear crystal; its foundation was garnished with divine wisdom, peace, and joy. At the first watch during the burst of glory clouds, we were asked to order for our diet: tranquillity dashed with honey dew, and a side of celestial melon.

While we embellished ourselves with the delicacies of the immortal city, angels would check out groups of redeemed humans known as the new race of immortals. My new body was exceptionally light; this weightless vessel was profoundly fast. I travelled at the speed of light one moment in eternity to rescue a young Chinese girl who I thought was in trouble with a mountain lion. I had forgotten that harming someone or something was a thing for time consciousness. There was no place in the new immortal city for hurt or pain.

Chapter 7
Immortalization Initiation

Moments eternalized as we were transported by a Cherubim to the wing folding centre. There we experienced what you might call 'night time'; no darkness, but a sense of stillness and reverence to the eternal moment.

The wing folding ceremony was splendorous. All the angels folded their wings to create a canopy over the Throne of the newly crown King of kings. All immortals were told to kneel and face the throne. We were given crowns, but not allowed to put them on during this period of quiet worship.

The feeling of gratefulness overwhelmed me so much until there was no strength found to lift my immortalized hands as I was commanded by Gabriel. I was told this was the initiation of our immortalization.

Finally all immortals were directed to cast their crowns at the feet of the eternal father of all immortals. I found myself very close to the feet of this glorious King. Everything in my body turned to corruption. I could not help but notice the scars that were so obviously pronounced in his feet; they appeared to have been burnt by a slow fire. I felt a gentle touch on my shoulder; it was commanding but refreshing. He lifted me up by his strong hand, and in his hands I felt weightless.

Indescribable was the moment of union. Truly He spoke to me, and then through his strength I was made strong, I am unable to explain my emotions during this time of refreshing. The words that He spoke were: *"My son welcome to forever-ness! Everything we do here is forever"*.

His voice sounded like sweet rest, yet it sounded like a peaceful river. I finally found the courage to look upward; my eyes met His profoundly laced with grace and compassion.

No angel or immortal was able to stand in His presence without the posture of worship. Not because He was ridged, but for the reverence of His majestic deportment. He did not only exude divine love and joy, but there was about Him a freshness that lingered eternally.

In the absence of time, the eternal existence was neither progressive nor static; it just simply is… Being in His presence was immortalizing. Reverential is inadequate to describe the moment of truth. Truly His presence was invigorating.

I chose my words very carefully. That majestic moment was invaluable. Finally I asked, "How long will we be with you in this capricious moment?" His voice tranquilized my unstable emotions. His reply was gracious and promisingly revealed: *"Haven't I told you in the ancient manuscript that I will forever be with you and you with me"*?

He stretched out his hands to embrace me as a good and caring father would during times of fearful encounters. I noticed the print of the nails in His scared palms. Immediately I felt the love emanating from His person, so much so until I realized no further questions were needed.

The River Of Life
At that segment of my eternal experience, a group of orderly angels came and took me to the most beautiful river I had ever seen. It looked like a sheet of glass because of her stillness. The reflection of the vastness of glory above it was almost breath-taking rather breath-giving. I was told this was the River Of Life and every immortal was required to drink from its stream. Hundreds of thousands were present for the drinking ceremony.

Immortals were gathered from every kindred and every tongue to participate in the cleansing of the mortal consciousness. This process was to further stimulate our immortalization.

Tree Of Life – Consciousness Reversed
On the other side of the river stood the most humongous tree I had ever laid eyes on. We were told it was the Tree Of Life. All immortals were given a leaf from the tree of life. We were directed to use it to draw water from the river. I followed the instructions and for a brief moment it felt like I had experienced a reversal in consciousness. Everything I had ever done flashed through my consciousness and then vanished.

Gazing through the corners of my eyes, I saw every Immortal behind and in front of me kneeling in uniformity. The finalization of memory eradication was completed. All previous bad memory was destroyed, and there was a separation of impure thoughts and pure thoughts. Impurities found a place in the abyss of the human race, but everything pure found its abode in the new celestial city.

Chapter 8

The Reward Ceremony

The atmosphere was blanketed with the sound of many waters. The celestial city was awakened by the voice of our leader; the one who had put all things under his feet. His majesty summoned everyone to his throne. Angels were directed to arrange spacing for all immortals. I turned and ask my guiding angel what was going on? He said, "We were being prepped for the reward ceremony".

All immortals were placed on the right side of the King of glory. His robe was blindingly white. The festival of colours that covered his majestic chair just seemed so unreal. I had to check my cognitive abilities to be assured that I was not dreaming. It was not a dream but an eternal moment that had no bearing on time.

During this period of intense scrutiny of all immortals, we were given our reward in direct proportion to our work in the time belt. All the angels lifted their wings upward and said, "Worthy is the Lamb to receive honour, power and glory".

Finally they stood in awe and admiration of the immortals. These heavenly beings had not experienced the joy and pain of being human. Furthermore they were inexperienced as it relates to our redemptive process.

The reward ceremony was one for the flash drive of eternity or the hard drive of the eternal archives. Each immortal was presented with a robe; it was not physical. When the immortals put on the robe of righteousness they experienced a rewarding felling of worthiness.

His majesty dressed each transformed human and said to those righteous recipients:

"Well done thou good and faithful servants, thou has been faithful over a few things, now I will make you ruler over many things; enter thou into the joy of thy Lord".

My Robe Of Righteousness
When it was my time to be dressed with this precious eternal commodity, I was forever grateful. His Lordship beckoned to me to approach His throne. Immediately feelings of joy and accomplishments permeated my entire being. I found myself prostrated before His Lordship. Surprisingly the protective Cherubim lifted me up to my feet and said, "This reward must be received by standing on your feet".

I lifted my eyes toward the conquering Lion of Judah, the one who relieved us and delivered us from the terrifying torment of death. When He opened His mouth there was a sound of many notes that vibrated deep inside our sanctified immortal souls.

Upon approaching His Majesty, I felt the space surrounding His throne filled with the oil of joy; every immortal that approached His throne was imbued with this divine radiance. A posture of worship was instantaneously taken.

THANK YOU LORD!
My experience was no different. I was endowed with the *robe of righteousness* right between a lingering gulp of laughter and a burst of worship. In my immortal spirit I felt a barrage of *THANK YOU LORD!* This feeling of appreciation was shared by all who were redeemed by our leader, who left His majestic throne in search of a lost world.

CHAPTER 9

My New Place of "Soul Rest"

When the initiation of our immortalization was completed, we were taken by a group of Gabriellites to a special place by the eastern gate. This special place was called 'Soul Rest' because of the softness of its welcoming atmosphere.

As we entered the eastern gate, I quickly recognized the name that was engraved on this particular gate. It was crafted in gold and laced with sapphire. St Peter was the recipient of this gate. Gabriel pointed us to a special group of redeemed immortals being taught by a once great Apostle who died the death of a martyr. To my surprised his saint-hood had afforded him the opportunity to lecture on the subject of *'Eternal Protocol.'*

Training For Reigning
Only Immortals were allowed to participate in this experience. I was selected to join this group of immortals in receiving *Training For Reigning*. Saint Peter was very hospitable considering his

previous personality. We were taught to cast our crowns and kneel when in the presence of His majesty. The newly crown king was extremely gracious to all immortals.

The atmosphere was always charged for worship. During this period of eternal worship all immortals were required to cast their crowns and bow their knees to the King of kings. In the presence of this highly spiritualized leader there was a vibration which caused every angel and transformed human to revere His presence. St Peter taught the immortals the importance of worship. In this new reality worship was not what we do, but who we are. My realization of the new paradigm was one of joy and fulfilment.

In the ancient manuscript we were prepared to experience paradise. Instead we got paradise squared. We were asked to get use to our eternalized bodies. Instead, we were taken to a secluded area where all immortals were told to exercise our deathlessness. To exercise one's deathlessness was to be sure of his eternalness. The indestructible body was one to be admired because of the vastness of its knowledge base.

We knew all things because of our conscious connection to the infinite mind of our Creator. In this new realization there was no time for contemplating. The information we needed to function was not to be recalled, for to recall was an action for the old consciousness.

A New State Of 'Now-ness'
We lived in a state of 'now-ness'. Our minds were always present. This state of being is only possible because we now live in his eternal presence, hence causing us to remain in a state of 'forever-ness'.

Night or day, sickness or wellness, good or bad, sleep or awake, having to choose whether we should do one or the other was something for the old consciousness. We were finally free from all those alienated thoughts, actions and experiences.

Living in this experience cannot be fully explained, because it has to be lived to understand the joy that is so real until it feels like it could be cut with a knife.

All the animals were eternity ready. The lions were friendly with the deer. They no longer saw the deer as dinner but as equal. There was a sense of equality that enveloped everyone and everything.

In the new reality there is no progression of time, because time was a well spent former commodity. In the eternal scheme of things, the Creator always desired that His people would be eternalized. In the time belt, choice was given to the human creation to reveal the righteousness of our leader - the King of all kings and Lord of all lords.

READ THESE QUOTES AND GET INSPIRED!

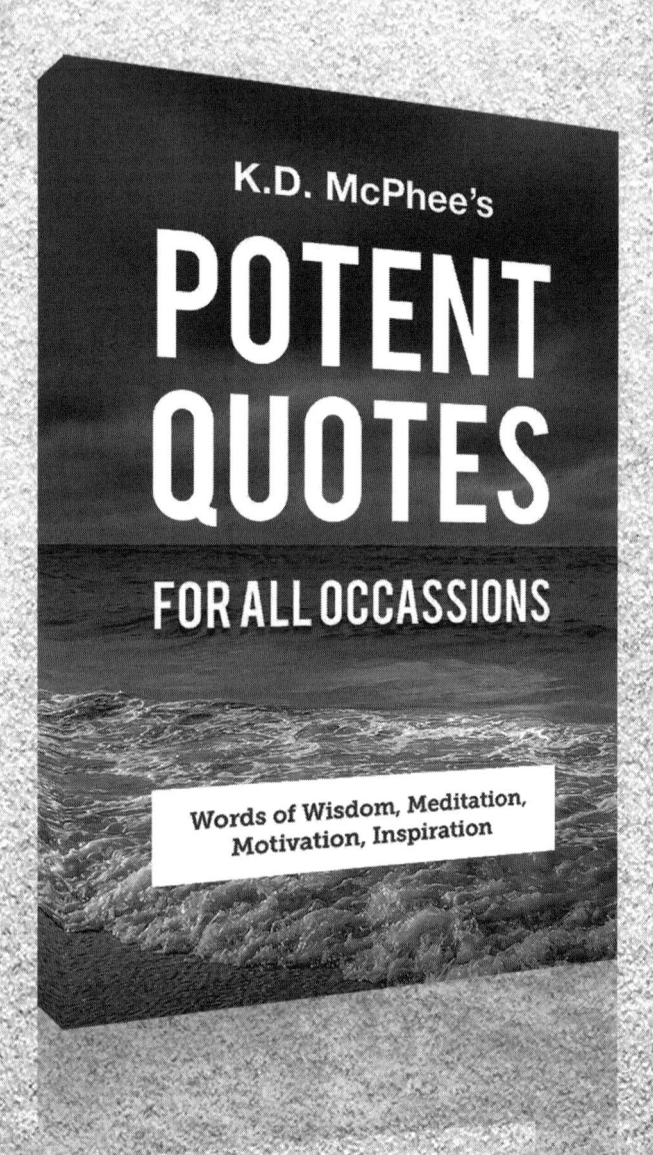

K.D. McPhee's

POTENT QUOTES

FOR ALL OCCASSIONS

Words of Wisdom, Meditation, Motivation, Inspiration

AVAILABLE FOR PURCHASE NOW!!!

Made in the USA
Middletown, DE
25 February 2021